THE FIDDLE-PLAYING FOX

Hank THE COWDOG

THE FIDDLE-PLAYING FOX

John R. Erickson

Illustrations by Gerald L. Holmes

Maverick Books
Published by Gulf Publishing Company
Houston, Texas

Maverick Books
Published by Gulf Publishing Company
P.O. Box 2608 Houston, Texas 77252-2608

C   D   E   F   G   H

Library of Congress Cataloging-in-Publication Data

Erickson, John R., 1943—
    [Hank the Cowdog and the case of the fiddle-playing fox]
    The fiddle-playing fox / John R. Erickson; illustrations by Gerald L. Holmes.
        p.   cm.
    At head of title: Hank the Cowdog.
    Previously published as: Hank the Cowdog and the case of the fiddle-playing fox.
    "The twelfth exciting adventure in the Hank the Cowdog series."
    Summary: While working on a mysterious case involving disappearing eggs and a fiddle-playing fox named Frankie, Hank the cowdog falls for Miss Beulah, the beautiful collie.
    ISBN 0-87719-169-7. —ISBN 0-87719-170-0 (pbk.)
    1. Dogs—Fiction. [1. Dogs—Fiction. 2. Mystery and detective stories. 3. Humorous stories. 4. West (U.S.)—Fiction.]
I. Holmes, Gerald L., ill. II. Title.
PS3555.R285H285   1990
813'.54—dc20
[Fic]
                                                    90-20315
                                                    CIP
                                                    AC

Printed in the United States of America.

Contents

Contents

CHAPTER
1
WHY THE SUN RISES, IN CASE YOU DIDN'T KNOW

It's me again, Hank the Cowdog. You're probably wondering what I was doing in bed at 8 o'clock on the morning of whatever day it is about which I'm fixing to speak.

It was in September, seems to me. Hot, still days, nights with just a hint of autumn chill. Kind of a lonesome time of year in these parts.

Yes, it was in September that I first heard about the Mysterious Fiddle Music in the night. Little did I know that very soon our hen house would be attacked by a devious, sneaking, outlaw rogue, or that I myself would become a suspect in the case, or that I would soon cross paths with the One Love of My Life, the incomparable, incredible Miss Beulah the collie.

But I'll get to that in a minute. I had mentioned something about sleeping late.

Ordinarily I take great pride in being the first one up on the ranch, don't you know. For one thing, I like to get a head start on everybody else. For another, I've never had complete confidence that the sun would come up without me there to supervise.

You want to know why I don't trust the sun? Simple logic.

The sun is round, right? A ball. If you've ever observed a sunrise, you've noticed that the sun is moving from the bottom of the sky to the top of the sky. In others words, this ball which we call the sun is *rolling uphill.*

It ain't natural for a ball, any ball, to roll uphill. In fact, it's impossible. Balls do not roll uphill unless, of course, they're urged along by an extraordinary outside force.

Now, I wouldn't want to come right out and say that I happen to be that extraordinary outside force which barks the sun up into the sky every day of the world and prevents total blackness from enveloping the globe.

On the other hand, I can't name anybody else on this outfit who does it, and if cold hard logic singles me out as the Bringer of Light and the Creator of Days . . .

A guy hates to toot his own horn, so to speak, but if you want to say that I'm the one who causes the sun to rise every day, I guess that's okay with me.

Where was I? Oh yes. After saying what I just said about me never EVER sleeping late, I'm going to give you a little shock by revealing that on a certain morning in September . . .

It was very warm, see, and sometimes on warm lazy mornings even I am tempted by the weaknesses of the flesh. When flesh gets warm, it develops a certain craving for things that are soft and even warmer, such as warm gunny sack beds.

And I can't always control my own flesh.

Oh, I know all the smart remarks you can make about late sleepers. "Studies show that more dogs die in bed than on streets and highways." Ho, ho. And, "What are you doing, trying to homestead that gunny sack?" Ha, ha. And, "Have you put down any roots in that bed?" Hee, hee.

Very funny. I slept late that morning and I don't care what anybody says about it and I don't feel guilty about it either. So there you are. You've got to be tough in this business.

Well, when I realized what I had . . . what my flesh had done, that is, I jumped up from

G.L. Holmes

my gunny sack, threw an arch in my back, took a big stretch, opened my mouth to its fully extended position, threw a curl into my tongue, and yawned.

I don't know that I had ever experienced a better yawn in my whole career. Wonderful. I love to yawn.

I looked down at my assistant. To no one's surprise, he was still asleep. "Get up, Half-Stepper, the day's half over. Are you trying to homestead that gunny sack?"

He had been twitching and grunting in his sleep. Now his eyes fell open, revealing for the first time the huge nothingness behind them.

"Irk mirk snicklefritz."

"That's no excuse. Wake up and let's get this day started."

"Irk snickle I am amirk. I never did go to snork last night."

"What?"

"I said," his eyes began to focus, "I am awake, I never did go to sleep last . . . or did I?"

"You did, take my word for it, and you might have even put down some roots in that gunny sack. Now GET UP!"

He sprang to his feet. "I'm up, I'm up! And

don't yell at me in the morning, you know what it does to me."

"I know that your shameful behavior has just won you a big fat goose egg."

"Oh boy, I love eggs."

"Goose egg means zero. It means you've flunked your examination and have failed to come up with a good excuse for sleeping late."

"Oh drat."

"This will have to go into your record, of course. Did you realize, Drover, that studies show that more dogs died in bed last year than on all the streets and highways in Ochiltree County?"

"No, I didn't know that."

"A bed is one of the most dangerous devices ever invented. It's been linked to thousands upon thousands of deaths."

"I'll be derned. What did they do with all the dead dogs?"

"We don't have an answer to that question yet, Drover, but the important point here is that there is an irreguffable relationship between *bed* and *dead*."

"Yeah, they rhyme."

"Exactly, so let that be a lesson to you. The next time you want to sleep until noon, you'd be better off and safer to sleep on a rattlesnake than on a bed."

"What time did you get up?"

"Eh, me? Well, uh, 5:30, as always. Or was it 4:30? Yes, it was 4:30. Very early. Before the chickens. As always."

At that very moment, whom do you suppose came pecking along our dog trail between the gas tanks and the corrals? *Pecking* is the clue here, and it rules out Pete the Barncat and other suspects who don't peck.

It was J. T. Cluck, the Head Rooster. He appeared to be pecking for seeds and gravel and the other garbage that chickens eat. He walked up to me and Drover, stared at the end of my tail, and then pecked it.

I don't appreciate anyone pecking my tail. It's not that I can't stand pain or that chickens are capable of inflicting much pain with their teakless booths—their toothless beaks, I should say. It's more a matter of principle. I just don't allow anyone to mess with my tail, that's all.

And so it should come as no surprise that after changing the location of my tail so the chicken couldn't peck it again, I snarled at him. That got his attention!

His head shot up so fast that it caused his comb, or whatever you call that red thing on his head, to jiggle. He squawked, flapped his wings, and jumped into the air.

"*Bawk-ka-bawk-bawk!* Elsa, Elsa, come quick!" He stared at me and blinked his eyes. "Well I'll be a son of a gun, was that your tail? I'm proud to see you dogs finally got out of bed."

Drover piped up. "Hank was up at 4:30 this morning. He told me so himself."

"Hush, Drover."

J. T. leaned forward and brought his beak about an inch from the end of Mister Big Mouth's nose. "Well, he told you a big fat lie! When I made first call this morning, your friend Hank was growing roots in that gunny sack right there."

"I . . . I'm afraid I don't know what you're talking about," I said.

"'Course you know what I'm talking about. I made first call before daylight and I seen you down here, sleeping your life away, beats anything I ever saw."

"You must have been mistaken."

"And when I made second call, you was still homesteading that gunny sack bed. Did you

8

know that more dogs died in bed last year than on all the streets and highways in Ochiltree County?"

I gave him a withering glare. "Where did you hear that? Have you been listening to our conversations?"

"Naw. I ain't ever been that hard up for something to do."

"In that case, I think you'd better scram. If there's anything I can't stand, it's a smart-aleck rooster first thing in the morning."

"If you ask me, sleeping late is more danger-ous than . . . ."

"BEAT IT!" I barked in his face. He squawked, flapped his wings, and went scurry-ing up the hill.

"Okay for you, mister," J.T. yelled over his wing, "and just for that, I ain't going to tell you about the Mysterious Fiddle Music in the Night!"

"That's fine with me, Featherbed, because . . . ."

HUH? Fiddle . . . in the . . . ?

And so the mystery began, with a careless statement by J.T. Cluck, the Head Rooster. At the time, I had no idea that it would lead me into new adventures and dangerous encounters with one of the slickest, smoothest, fiend-ishest crinimal characters I had ever encountered.

If I had known it, I don't know what I would have done, but chances are that I would have done something, because even doing nothing is something.

Not much, but still something.

C H A P T E R

2

LITTLE ALFRED'S
SCHOOL OF CAT ROPING

I looked at Drover. "What did he just say?"
The question caught him in the middle of a
yawn. "What? Who?"

"That rooster. He just said something over
his shoulder."

"I didn't know chickens had shoulders."

"Over his wing!"

"Oh. Yeah, I think he did say something—
about a gigantic fiddleback spider in the
night."

"Hmmm. That's funny." Suddenly Drover
began laughing. I stared at him. "What's so
funny?"

"I don't know, but you said it was funny
and all at once I thought it was funny, too, and
I guess . . . well, I couldn't help laughing."

I narrowed my eyes and studied the wasteland of his face. "Are you trying to make a mockery of my investigation?"

"No, I just . . . couldn't help . . . laughing . . . is all."

"Well, this is no laughing matter, so wipe that stupid grin off your face." He wiped it off.

"That's better. Now, let's start all over again. What did J. T. Cluck say? It was something about a fiddle."

Drover rolled his eyes and chewed his lip. "Fiddle. Fiddle? Fiddle. I'll be derned, I just drew a blank."

"You drew a blank the day you were born, Drover, and it settled between your ears. Concentrate and try to remember. Fiddle."

"Fiddle. Oh yeah. He said he woke up in the night and saw a gigantic fiddleback spider crawling into the chicken house. I think that's what he said."

"That's NOT what he said."

"I didn't think it was."

"He said he heard Mysterious Fiddle Music in the Night."

"Oh yeah, and the spider was playing the fiddle behind his back."

"He said nothing about a spider."

"I didn't think he did."

"So we can forget about the spiders."

"Oh good."

"But we can't forget about the Mysterious Music."

"No, it kind of gets in your head."

"Which means that we have an unconfounded report from an unreliable source about Mysterious Fiddle Music in the Night. Hence, the next question is, do we dismiss it as hearsay and gossip, or do we follow it up with a thorough investigation?"

"That's a tough one."

"And the answer to that question, Drover, is very simple."

"That's what I meant."

"We follow it up with a complete and thorough investigation, because to do otherwise would be a dare election of duty."

"I'll vote for that."

I began pacing. As I might have noted before in another context, my mind seems to work better when I pace.

"Question, Drover. Do you know anything about this so-called Mysterious Fiddle Music in the Night?"

He flopped down and started scratching his left ear. "Well, let's see here. Fiddle music. I always kind of liked fiddle music, myself."

"Yes? Go on."

"Especially when they play fast. It gets me all stirred up."

"Get to the point."

"The point. Okay, let's see here." All at once his eyes got big and his mouth dropped open. "Say, you know what? I dreamed about fiddle music last night!"

I whirled around and paced over to a point directly in front of him. "All right, very good, we're getting to the core of the heart. You say that you dreamed about fiddle music last night?"

"Yeah, I sure . . . unless . . . gosh, maybe I didn't dream it. Maybe . . . there was this fox, came out of nowhere and stood over me while I was asleep. And Hank, he was playing a fiddle!"

I let the air hiss out of my lungs and my eyelids sank. "Okay, never mind, I'm sorry I asked, I should have known better."

"Did I say something wrong?"

I refilled my lungs and raised my lids. "I thought we were on the trail of something, Drover, but it's turned out to be another of your wild, improbable fantasies. Number one, there are no foxes on this ranch."

"Oh dern."

"Number two, even if there were a fox on this ranch, which there isn't, he wouldn't be playing a fiddle because foxes don't play fiddles."

"Huh. Maybe it was a harmonica."

"Number three, you're wasting my valuable time. I don't want to hear anymore about foxes or fiddles or spiders."

"But Hank . . . ."

"Period. End of discussion. Now, what were we doing before that rooster intruded into our lives and got us stirred up about nothing?"

"Sleeping, I think."

"Wrong again, Drover. YOU were sleeping. I had been up since before daylight, checking things out and getting the day started. Speaking of which, the day has started and we have two weeks of work to do before dark."

Just then I heard the screen door slam up at the house. Hmm. Oftentimes the slamming of the screen door at that hour of the morning indicates that Sally May has come outside to distribute juicy morsels of food left over from breakfast.

"Come on, Drover. Never mind the work, it's scrap time! To the yard gate, on the double."

We went streaking up the hill, just in time to

see Pete the Barncat scampering towards the yard gate. No doubt he too had heard the screen door slam, and he, being your typical ne'er-do-well, freeloading, never-sweat variety of cat, had been lurking in the flowerbeds, waiting for someone to come out and give him a free meal.

That's one trait in cats that has always burned me up. You'd think that a ranch cat, a barn cat, would feel some obligation to get out and hustle and earn his keep.

Not this one. He spent his entire life lurking around doors, and the instant he heard someone coming out, ZOOM! There he was, rubbing up against someone's leg and purring like a little motorboat and waiting for a handout.

It's disgusting, is what it is, and the worst part about it is that his handouts cut into our Food Rewards for Meritorious Service.

Don't let anyone kid you. There's a huge difference between mere handouts and Food Rewards, but never mind the difference because the sleen-scramming—screen-slamming, that is, turned out to be a false alarm anyway. For you see, the person or persons who had emerged from the house turned out to be Little Alfred, not Sally May as you might have suspected, which meant no scraps.

We skidded to a stop in front of the yard gate and waited for our pal, age four or thereabouts, to come out of the yard. He was wearing a pair of brown shorts, a T-shirt, and his little Tony Lama boots, with the spurs attached.

And in his hands was an instrument of mischief: a little three-sixteenth-inch nylon rope. And he was building a loop.

It's amazing what happens to Drover when someone shows a rope. He suddenly changes direction, drops his head, and begins slinking away.

Sure, he'd been roped a few times by cowboy pranksters and he didn't enjoy it, but so what? That was no reason for him to be a spoilsport and a chicken-liver about it. Shucks, if I'd had a bone for every time I'd been roped by Slim and Loper, I'd have been one of the 10 wealthiest dogs in the country.

But you didn't see me slinking away every time somebody showed up with a rope in his hands, and besides, I had reason to suspect that Little Alfred couldn't hit a bull in the behind with a bass fiddle, much less toss his loop around my neck.

Furthermore, there was always the chance that he might put on a little exhibition, with

Pete playing the part of livestock. Stranger things had happened, and I didn't want to miss a minute of it.

I mean, if you care about cowboying, you like to see these kids learning to rope and carrying on the skills into another generation, and when they're roping cats, it warms the heart even more.

Pete suspected nothing. That wasn't exactly the biggest surprise of the year since cats aren't what you'd call cowboy animals. They don't understand the business at all and have no idea of what goes on inside a cowboy's head.

We cowdogs, on the other hand, have a pretty good reading of a cowboy's mind, and one of the first principles we learn is that *a loaded rope tends to go off.*

But do you think Pete picked up on that? No sir. He went right on rubbing and purring and winding his tail around the boy's legs, I mean, it looked like a bullsnake climbing a tree.

Little Alfred stumbled over the cat, which is what usually happens. He stopped and looked down. A gleam came into his eyes and a smile spread across his mouth.

Up went the rope. Three twirls later, a nice little loop sailed out and dropped over Pete's head, just as pretty as you please.

G.C. Holmes

I barked, wagged my tail, and jumped up and down. I mean, I could hardly contain my pride and enthusiasm. Did I say the boy couldn't rope? Couldn't hit a bull in the behind with a bass fiddle? Fellers, he had just one-looped a cat, and I couldn't have been prouder if I'd done it myself!

Well, you know Pete, sour-puss and can't-take-a-joke. He pinned his ears down, growled, hissed, and made a dash for the iris patch. Ho ho! Did he come to a sudden stop? Yes he did. Hit the end of that twine, came to a sudden stop, and did a darling little back flip.

Little Alfred beamed a smile at me. "I woped a cat!"

I barked and wagged and gave him my most sincere congratulations on a job well done.

He reeled the cat in. By this time, old Pete had quit fighting the rope and had sulled up. His ears were still pinned down and he was making that police-siren growl that cats make when they ain't real happy about the state of the world.

Alfred picked him up, opened the gate, and joined me on the other side, guess he wanted to show me his trophy. I gave him a big juicy lick on the face and was about to . . . .

HUH?

The little snipe! Now, why did he go and pitch the cat on me? Hey, I'd been on his side all along. I'd been out there cheering him on and trying to coach . . . .

All at once, Pete wasn't sullen anymore. He'd turned into a buzz saw, and before I even knew what was happening, he'd stung me in fifteen different places, and we're talking about very important places such as my eyebrows, cheeks, gums, lips, ears, and the soft part of my nose.

Did it hurt? You bet it hurt, and never mind who'd started this riot, I was fixing to introduce Pete to an old cowdog technique called "Disaster." I barked and I snarled and I growled and I snapped . . . .

"HANK, YOU BULLY, GET AWAY FROM MY CAT!!"

Huh?

Get away from . . . no doubt that voice belonged to Sally May and . . . perhaps she thought . . . .

I cancelled my plans for hamburgerizing the cat, and prepared to thump my tail on the ground and give her an innocent smile.

At the time, I didn't know that she was already upset about the missing eggs. But I soon found out.

C H A P T E R

3

THE CASE OF THE MISSING EGGS

S he came storming down the hill, carrying the egg bucket in her left hand. Right hand. Who cares?

Carrying the egg bucket in one hand and with the other she held Baby Molly. No doubt the two of them had been up at the chicken house, gathering eggs. (That explained the egg bucket, see.)

She reached the bottom of the hill and set the egg bucket down on the ground beside me. Naturally, I peered inside and gave the bucket a sniffing, with no thought or intention of . . . some dogs will eat eggs, don't you see, and they're known as Egg-Sucking Dogs and they ain't popular with ranch wives or whoever else is in charge of the . . . .

Nothing could have been further from my mind. Honest. Cross my heart and hope to die. I have flaws, but sucking eggs has never been one of them, although I must admit that at certain times of the day and certain times of the year, a nice fresh egg . . . .

She speared me with her eyes. "Don't you even THINK about messing with my eggs!"

Who, me? Now, what had . . . all I'd . . . there was no reason to . . . .

Sometimes the best thing a guy can do is just keep his mouth shut and take a telling, even when it involves stuffing down his sense of mortal outrage. In the process of stuffing down the so forth, I sniffed again. It was just a mannerism, it meant nothing at all, but Sally May took it all wrong and turned it into something that was blown all out of . . . .

"Stop smelling my eggs because they're not for you!"

Okay, okay. But for what it's worth, they smelled pretty good, although that wasn't my primary . . . .

Let me repeat that I am not now and never have been an egg-sucking dog, and that's my last word on the subject. For a while.

At that moment, High Loper came up the hill. He'd been down at the barn doing his morning chores, which at that time of the year meant feeding one saddle horse and a two-year-old colt. The rest of the horses were grazing on grass.

He walked up to us, swept his eyes over me, the cat, and Little Alfred, and grinned. "Well, well, what do we have cooking here?"

Sally May placed both hands on her hips. "Your son and your dog. You see what they're doing?"

Little Alfred beamed, as all eyes turned to him. "I woped me a cat, Daddy."

"Yes," Sally May went on, "he roped my poor cat and then threw him on your dog, just to see what would happen."

Loper chuckled. "What happened?"

"You know very well what happened. If I hadn't come down just when I did, Hank would have brutalized the cat."

"From the looks of the blood, hon, it was the other way around. It looks like your cat brutalized my poor dog."

She glanced down at me. I wagged my tail extra hard. I was disappointed to see her smile. "He did take a few licks, didn't he, but I'm sure he deserved them. Now, will you speak to your son about starting cat-and-dog fights?"

Loper knelt down and gave Alfred a lecture

about roping cats and starting fights, although I got the feeling that Loper might have participated in the same sports when he was young.

"Oh," said Sally May, "and while we're on the subject of your dog, I found seven broken eggs in the chicken house this morning. *Something* got in there last night," she turned a dark glare in my direction, "and is eating my eggs."

I turned away, astonished that she might think . . . .

Loper stood up, and as usual his knees popped three times. "Now hold on. What makes you think Hank had anything to do with it?"

"Well . . . I don't know. Nothing really, except that he has a lousy reputation around here, and anytime there's a mess or some trouble, he's a prime suspect."

Her words cut me to the crick. It was really tough to sit there and listen to such falsehoods and never say a word in my own defense. I managed to keep silent, but just barely.

"I doubt that Hank's the culprit, hon. More than likely, it was a skunk or a bullsnake, but just because you're such a sweet and gorgious thang, I'll go up and check it out."

He gave her a kiss on the cheek.

"Well, that's nice. Thank you. I'll be much sweeter and more gorgious if I can get my twelve eggs a day."

With that, she herded her two children into the yard, un-noosed the cat, and disarmed Little Alfred. Loper and I went up the hill to chick out the checking house. Chicken house. Check out the chicken house.

As we passed the big sliding doors of the machine shed, whose nose do you suppose poked out of the crack between the doors? It was Mister Scared-He'll-Get-Roped.

"Hi Hank, looks like we might get some rain, huh?" I ignored him, so naturally he came out and fell in step beside me. "Where we going?"

"I don't know where *you're* going, but Loper and I are going to the chicken house on important business."

"Oh good."

"But I'd just as soon not be seen with you, after the way you ran from that rope."

"Yeah, that was quite a rope."

By this time, Loper had reached the chicken house. He pushed open the big door on the east. The chickens never used this door, for the simple reason that chickens are unable to turn doorknobs and push open large doors. They came and went through a small opening near the center of the building.

I was already studying the layout of the alleged chicken house, committing every detail of its construction to memory, amassing facts and clues, and sending it all to Data Control. A guy never knows which tiny fact will be the one that breaks a case wide open.

Loper stepped inside, causing the hens to squawk and flutter. I followed one step behind, put my nose to the floor and began . . . .

You ever try to sniff out a scent in a chicken house? You should try it sometime, just put your nose to the floor and take a deep breath. When you regain consciousness, you'll realize that even an elephant could hide his scent in a chicken house.

My nose is a very sensitive smellatory instrument, see, and it's calibrated to pick up SUBTLE odors. There are many odors in a chicken house, none of them subtle. One whiff of that place blew out all my circuits.

When I stopped coughing, I was able to mutter, "Boy, this is a foul place!"

"Yeah," said Drover, "they're just birds."

"What?"

G. L. Holmes

"I said, fowls are just birds. That's how come they're in a chicken house."

Sometimes . . . oh well. I had more important things to do than to make sense of Drover's nonsense.

Loper was bending over one of the nests, which was located inside a wooden crate. I hopped up and studied the contents of the nest. There, lying amidst the straw, were pieces of egg shell.

Loper moved on down the line and found other nests with broken eggs. Then he straightened up, worked a kink out of his back, and pushed his straw hat to the back of his head.

"Well, dogs, something's been robbing these nests." I barked. Now we were getting somewhere. "It wasn't a bullsnake, because a snake wouldn't have left the shells in the nest."

"It looks like the work of a skunk, but if it had been a skunk, he would have left a scent behind. That leaves a coon or a coyote. The next question is, where were you fools when the coyote or coon came into headquarters?"

Huh? Well, it was a big ranch and . . . .

"Let's just say that if I find anymore busted eggs, I might start thinking about my dog food bill. I might just run the cost of gain on you mutts and decide to cut down on my overhead."

He leaned down and brought his face real close to mine. "Do you understand what I'm saying? No more busted eggs. No more angry wife. No more varmints in the chicken house. Tend to your business!"

Tend to . . . what did he think we'd . . . but, yes, the message had come through loud and clear, so loud and so clear that I left the chicken house shaking all over.

If you happen to be a dog, the prospect of life without dog food can be rather bleak. We had a job to do, fellers, and we dared not fail.

CHAPTER
4

THE CASE OF THE PHONEY FIDDLE MUSIC IN THE NIGHT

Loper closed the door, gave us one last scorching glare, and stomped back down to the corrals. Needless to say, I had little desire to go with him. There are times to be a loyal dog and there are times to be invisible. I choose invisible.

As soon as Loper's footsteps faded into the distance, I turned to my assistant. "Well, you sure made a mess of this deal. Where were you last night when the robber strolled into the chicken house and had himself a feast?"

"I don't know. I never saw him."

"Exactly. Now, the next question is, why didn't you see him? What were you doing that

33

was more important than guarding the chicken house?"

"Well . . . ."

"Nothing. That's the answer. Nothing was more important than guarding the chicken house, and that is precisely what you were doing."

"Oh. Well, I guess I was doing the right thing, huh?"

"Absolutely wrong."

"Oh drat. But Hank, if nothing was more important than guarding the chicken house, then I was doing the more important thing, seems to me."

I glared at him. "Are you trying to confuse me?"

"Not really."

"Good. It would be a waste of your time to try. Furthermore . . . ."

At that moment I realized that I was being stared at by a pair of rooster eyes—at close range. You ever been stared at by a rooster at close range? They have this funny way of twisting their heads, see, and blinking their eyes, as if they're not sure what it is they're looking at.

As you might have guessed, J. T. Cluck had

returned—without being invited, I might add.

"Oh, it's you again, " said J.T. "I was a-wondering what that was. Did you just come out of the chicken house?"

"Who wants to know?"

"Who do you think, you darn fool dog? ME! I want to know who's going in and out of my chicken house. You may not know it, mister, and you may not care, but we've been losing eggs in the night."

"I'm aware of that, and as a matter of fact, I just happen to be working on the case at this very moment."

"Huh. Somehow that don't thrill me the way it ort to."

"Oh yeah? Well, thrilling chickens ain't something I'd care to do, even if I didn't have anything else on my agenda, which I do. But while you're here and wasting my time anyway, I might as well ask you a few questions."

"Go ahead, ask me some questions, ask me anything. My life's an open book."

"I know. And if you had to make your living selling it, you'd starve to death."

"Say what? What's that supposed to mean?"

"Nothing." I fixed him with a stern gaze and began to pace back and forth in front of him.

Did I mention that my mind works better when I . . . yes, I did. "All right, let's get down to the brass tacks."

"Fine, I'm ready, ask me anything. Say, you ever been pecking for gravel and swaller a brass tack? I did that once, and you talk about indigestion! That was the first time in my life that I ever got cavities in my gizzard gravel."

"That's very interesting."

"Yeah, I know. We ain't got teeth, maybe you didn't realize that. We swaller gravel and it goes down to the gizzard and the gizzard grinds up our food."

"Yes, I know."

"So we never have problems with our teeth, see. You can't have problems with what you ain't got."

"I'm very happy for you but . . . ."

"Pretty good system most of the time, but like Elsa says, she says a rooster my age has got no business swallering tacks and nails and running all that hardware through my gizzard."

"J.T.?"

"Causes cavities in the gizzard gravel and gives me indigestion."

"Tell me about last night."

"Huh? Last night? Naw, this happened

36

several weeks ago.''

''Never mind your indigestion. What happened last night? Did you see or hear anything out of the ordinary?''

''Well, let me think here.'' He cocked his head and raised one foot off the ground. ''Yes, I did. I heard something last night that I won't forget for a long time.''

''Okay, tell me about it. Describe exactly what you heard and keep to the facts.''

''You bet, here we go. You know what was strange about the whole deal?'' He glanced over both wings and moved closer. ''What was funny about that deal of the busted eggs was that sometime in the deep dark of the night, I woke up—I was on the roost, see, sleeping real good—I woke up in the deep dark of the night and heard . . . .''

I stood motionless, waiting to hear the rest. ''Yes? You heard something? Go on.''

''Naw, you wouldn't believe it.''

''Try me.''

''Naw, it's just too outrageous, and I ain't sure I believe it my own self.''

''TELL ME WHAT YOU HEARD!''

''Well, you don't have to screech, I ain't deaf yet! Okay, I'll tell you the rest of the

darned story. I woke up in the deep dark of the night and I heard something. And what I heard was . . . fiddle music!''

"Fiddle music?"

"Yes sir, that's exactly what I heard. Fiddle music."

I swung my eyes around to Drover. He was looking up at the clouds. "Have you been talking to this rooster behind my back?"

His gaze drifted down and settled on me. It was as empty a gaze as I'd ever seen. "Oh, hi. I was just watching the clouds. Kind of looks like rain."

"Never mind the rain. This rooster says he heard fiddle music last night."

"I'll be derned, so did I."

"That's quite a coincidence, wouldn't you say? Two unreliable witnesses making the same outrageous claim on the same day?"

"Sounds pretty crazy, all right."

"Exactly, that's my whole point. If only one of you had made such a claim, I might have passed it off as mere chance, but the fact that both of you told the same story points to something deeper and darker."

"Yeah, it makes you think we heard the same fiddle."

I couldn't help chuckling at his nativity . . .

niavity . . . naw-eev-ity . . . at his simple-minded response. "Except that there WAS no fiddle, Drover, and therefore no fiddle music. Now the question becomes, why would you and J. T. Cluck go to the trouble to tell me the same incredible yarn?"

"Oh, it wasn't any trouble."

I stuck my nose in his face. "Could it be that I have exposed a little conspiracy here? Perhaps you were bored and thought it would be fun to pull a practical joke on old Hank?"

"I don't think so."

"Tell him a crazy story about fiddle music in the night, get him stirred up and running off in all directions? Yes, of course. Nice try, Drover, you almost pulled it off, but you forgot one small detail."

"I did?"

"Yes. You got a rooster to corroborate your story, never realizing that you had picked the most unreliable witness on the entire ranch, never realizing that when interrogating chickens, I always use the Principle of Reversal."

"You do?"

"Exactly. Which means that to arrive at the truth, I reverse the chicken's testimony. Hence, if a chicken claims to have heard fiddle music, it means that he heard either a tuba or nothing at all."

"I'll be derned."

"So there you are. You walked right into my trap, Drover."

"Maybe it was tuba music."

Having unmasked Drover, I whirled around to expose J. T. Cluck. "And as for you, rooster . . . ." He was gone, so I whirled back around to Drover. "There, you see? Your partner in this little sham . . . ."

Hmmm. Drover was gone too, just vanished without a trace. I sat down on the gravel driveway and scratched a troublesome spot on my right ear.

Since I had never interrogated myself, I could only speculate on how J. T. and Drover must have felt as I bored into their tiny minds with my drill-bit questions. It must have been a terrifying experience, and who could blame them for running away at the first opportunity?

Sometimes I'm frightened by my own powers—those blinding flashes of insight that light up the dark night of darkness and iffumigate every crack and corner in the murky cellar of . . . something.

Well, I had wrapped up the Case of the Phoney Fiddle Music in the Night in what must have been near-record time. But the Case of the Broken Eggs hung over me like a dark cloud—a gloomy, rolling dark thundercloud that . . . .

Raindrops?

Rain?

Hard rain?

Pellets of hail?

Yikes, it was raining snakes and weasels, and also hailstones the size of . . . I made a dash for the machine shed, but not soon enough to escape getting drenched and peppered with hailstones.

Inside, I shook myself and sat down to watch the downpour. All at once, I began to feel that I was being watched. Very slowly, I turned my head on its pivotal mechanism and cast a glance to my right.

There, only a few feet away, sat J. T. Cluck and Drover.

Drover grinned. "I thought those clouds might do something."

"We was a-wondering," said J.T., "how long it would take you to come in out of that rain. It's like I told Elsa one time, I said, 'Elsa . . .' "

Never mind. I may have been all wet, but I would soon dry off. There was no cure for being a dumb chicken.

CHAPTER

5

THE DEADLY SHOWER
OF SPARKS

It was one of those sudden downpours that we get in the fall of the year. The clouds pile up in the . . . well, in the sky, of course, and all at once they open up and drop buckets of rain.

It's no disgrace to get caught out in one of those downpours because they come very suddenly and without any warning.

It rained hard for about 10 minutes. Then it stopped just as suddenly as it had come. The moment it stopped J. T. Cluck went streaking out of the machine shed. Something about getting the worms when they were out of their holes and worms being good for his digestion. Something like that. Not that I cared, you understand. I was glad to be rid of him, regardless of the reason.

I had planned to do a routine search for tracks and scent around the chicken house, on the slim chance that it might turn up a lead in the case. But the rain had taken care of that and had reduced my chances of finding anything to near zero.

"Well, Drover, it's pretty clear what must happen now."

"Yeah, the sun'll come out and before you know it, we'll be dry again."

"We've got no clues, no leads, no suspects. So far, it's been a dry run."

"Yeah, but every little bit of moisture helps."

"If you were in charge of things, what would be your next move?"

"Oh, I'd bring out the sun for a while and dry things out. Then I'd let it rain again."

I stared at him. "What?"

"Oh, I just said . . . I don't think I said anything."

"I thought I heard someone speak."

"Not me. I didn't say a word."

"Hmm, that's odd. I could have sworn . . . . Drover, this case has me stumped. I can't seem to find a handle."

He looked around in a circle. "No, there aren't many around here."

"Oftentimes, when we reach a dead-end in a case, the best way to proceed is with a radical departure, something that will blow the case wide open. If you agree with that, as I'm sure you will, then tonight at dark we will stake out the chicken house and wait for the villain to strike again."

"Who's *we*?"

"We, Drover, meaning the entire Security Division."

"Well, I don't know, Hank, I'm liable to be . . . ."

"We're going to throw all units into this case, and stay with it until we've got a suspect. I guess I don't need to tell you that this could get us into some combat. "

He stood up and began limping around in a circle. "You know, this change in the weather has sure done something to this old leg of mine. I don't know but what . . . ."

"A good long nap will fix you right up, Drover. Come dark, you'll be good as new."

"I don't know. This dampness . . . ."

"Try it, Drover. I'm sure it'll work. But just in case it doesn't, think about life without dog food."

"It does feel a little better, now that I've worked some of the soreness out."

"Good. Now let's get some shut-eye. I've cancelled all the afternoon's operations. Everything is on hold until we break this case. Good night, Drover. Or maybe I should say, good afternoon."

"I think it's still morning."

"Very well, good morning."

"Good night, Hank, I hope I can sleep with all this pain."

We curled up inside the machine shed and spent the entire afternoon throwing up long lazy lines of *Z*'s. It was a wonderful experience.

Oh, there were a few minor interruptions. The flies were bothersome, but we expect that in the fall and take certain corrective measures to reduce the nuisance factor. We're able to put our ears on Automatic Twitch, don't you know, and that pretty muchly takes care of the fly problem.

Then, sometime in the middle of the afternoon, Loper came blundering into the machine shed and spent half an hour running the high-speed grinder. I have no idea what he was doing over there—grinding on a piece of steel, I suppose, and it was very noisy, and after a while he must have gotten bored because he turned the grinder around so that it threw a shower of sparks on ME.

There are certain people in this world who can't stand to see someone else enjoying a peaceful sleep. It seems to bring out the very worst qualities in their nature. It turns them into maniacs and statistic pranksters. They won't take a hint, they won't go away, they won't quit tormenting the innocent party until the innocent party is dragged from the warm vapors of sleep.

I ignored him as long as I could. I mean, I was aware of what he was doing. I knew that tiny fragments of red hot metal were hitting the lower dorsal quadrant of my body. But I also knew that my hair would trap the sparks and allow them to cool before they made contact with my skin, which meant that I was fairly safe.

I knew what he wanted: a big explosive reaction from me. Maybe it was stubbornness on my part, but I didn't want to yield to his childish prank. Twice I raised up and gave him a long patient stare, and whapped my tail on the cement floor, as if to say, "Okay, you've had your fun. Now go away and leave me alone."

Do you think that was good enough for him? I'm telling you, these cowboys are childish beyond your wildest dreams. No sir, that wasn't good enough for him, and do you know what he did?

He bore down harder on that piece of steel, which caused the grinder to throw out sparks that were even bigger and hotter than the ones it had thrown out before, and it was only a matter of time until his infantile wish was granted.

Yes, at last one of the bigger and hotter fragments of steel burned through the outer protective layer of hair, dropped down to the skinalary region of my left dorsal hiney, and burned itself into the consciousness of my mind.

At which point I erupted from the warm vapors of sleep, leaped several feet in the air, screeched, and moved my business to the northwest corner of the machine shed, where I took up sleep between Loper's canvas-covered canoe and three dusty boxes that contained Christmas tree decorations.

As I passed Drover, he opened one eye, which resembled a single grape suspended in a bowl of red Jello, and muttered, "Murgle pork chop skittle ricky tattoo."

To which I made the only sensible reply: "Oh shut up!"

Well, judging by the amount of laughter that went up over by the grinder, Loper got a big kick out of his stupid, childish, infantile, stupid prank.

Oh yes, a big chuckle. In fact, at one point he sank to his knees and pounded the cement with his hands, while I glared daggers at him from the gloomy darkness of the machine shed and thought unkind thoughts about him.

As far as I could determine, the thought never entered his mind that he had intruded into the precious rebuilding and restoring time of the HEAD OF RANCH SECURITY.

Did it ever occur to him that soon, all too soon, I would be out on the front lines, alone in the darkness, facing some horrible trudging Thing of the Night? Providing his ranch with its First Line of Defense? Protecting HIS ranch, HIS chicken house, HIS wife's daily supply of eggs without which . . . .

Oh, no, none of that. He thought only of his own childish, infantile pleasures, and tormenting a poor, overworked, unappreciated dog and depriving him of his precious sleep.

Now, if he had done the same thing to Drover, that would have been a slightly different deal, seeing as how Drover is used primarily in a backup capacity and his role in the overall . . . but no, he chose ME as his victim and . . . oh well.

Sometimes the mind reels at the follies of this life.

Okay. At long last, Loper had his fill of childish follyrot and went back to . . . I almost said "work" but that might have been overly optimistic. He went back down to the corrals and did whatever it was that he had been doing before.

But the important thing was that he left me alone so that I could sleep and prepare my body for the deadly combat that almost certainly lay ahead of me.

At last I dropped off to sleep, but for the next four hours I dreamed of high-speed grinders and showers of sparks, and every time a fly landed upon my body, I twitched and groaned and waited to be scorched.

It was, to put it briefly, a fistful sleep. Fitful sleep, that is.

Then the moment came for awakening. I pushed myself up from the rags and shreds of cardboard upon which I had been forced to sleep. I saw the rays of the twilight sun pouring through the cracks in the big double doors.

And I knew that the time had come. In slumber, my life had marched on through time to the roll of the invisible drums, bringing me closer, ever closer, to the moment when I would face . . . .

Limbering up my body, doing a few callus-thinkus . . . calthelenics . . . callus—the freshly-awakened mind has trouble grasping big words—while going through several exercises to promote the flow of bodily fluids, I found myself wondering who HE was.

A deadly badger? A skunk, perhaps carrying rabies? A member of the wild coyote tribe? An enormous boar coon with teeth that could rip a dog to shreds?

And I wondered what he was doing at this very moment, what preparations he might be making for his slouch through the darkness, what thoughts were passing through the shadows of his mind.

I could only guess, and guessing about such matters seldom leads to happiness. In the end, I preferred ignorance over bliss, or whatever the old saying is.

I made my way through the gloom of the machine shed and called to Drover in a soft voice. "Drover, the moment has come. We are called to meet our fate in the night."

Didn't faze him, so I gave him a boot and yelled, "Get up, Half-Stepper, it's time to go to work!" That did the trick.

He staggered around in circles for a minute or two. And then we marched out into night's last day . . . day's last light, I should say, and began our lonely virgil.

CHAPTER

6

LONELINESS ON THE FRONT LINES

C rouched in some weeds across from the chicken house, we waited in the darkness and silence.

Did I say silence? Not exactly. A guy never realizes how much non-silence there is on a quiet autumn night until he's forced to sit and listen.

Crickets, for example. You ever stop and wonder how many crickets there are in this world? Neither had I, but there are bound to be bunches and bunches of crickets.

And did you ever stop and wonder how one cricket can make so much noise? I mean, we're talking about a little bitty feller who makes something more than a little bitty racket.

Don't crickets ever get tired? You'd think

so, but they go on and on, making their chirp or whatever it is, and they don't ever seem to sleep.

Well, after studying crickets for a lot longer than I ever wanted to, I came to the conclusion that whoever builds 'em is pretty handy with his tools.

And there were other sounds in the night. The hooting of an owl. The "voom" of bull-bats. The howling of coyotes. Bullfrogs saying, *"Rrrump, rrump!"* down on the creek.

And then there was the whisper of the wind. Did you know that the wind has a different voice for every season of the year? It does, and when you live outside, the way I do, you become something of an expert on the subject.

I listen to the wind every day and every night, and I can tell you that in the fall of the year, that old wind sings a lonesome song. It makes you wonder what happened to spring, and where the summertime went.

And that's the kind of song I was hearing, as I listened to the wind blowing through the trees. It went kind of like this.

Wind Song

She came here in the springtime
With flowers in her hair,
Inquiring for a place to stay
Until the trees grew bare.

I saw her in the cottonwoods,
Beneath their pools of shade.
She caught a puff of cotton
And blew it on its way.

Oh sing songs of sunshine,
Sing songs of rain,
Sing songs of springtime gone,
Sing them all again.

She stayed through the summer
  months,
I saw her having fun.
She took a gold strand of hair
And wrapped it 'round the sun.

She warmed the earth and kissed
  its face
With lips of sparkling dew.
I thought she'd stay forever,
Her name I never knew.

Oh sing songs of sunshine,
Sing songs of rain,
Sing songs of springtime gone,
Sing them all again.

The autumn came, I heard the
    wind
And saw the swirls of red,
And cottonwoods with gnarled
    limbs
Against a sky of lead.

I called for her to warm herself
And said that she must stay.
But all at once her eyes turned sad
And then she went away.

Oh sing songs of sunshine,
Sing songs of rain,
Sing songs of springtime gone,
Sing them all again.

Kind of mournful, huh? That old autumn
wind can sure send a chill or two down your
backbone, especially if you happen to be on a
dangerous assignment in the dead of night.

And there were other sounds I couldn't identify: whispers and rustles and clatters and snaps, swishes and sighs and moans and slithers. Those were the ones that made me uneasy because . . . . Well, a guy never knows what manner of beast might produce that kind of noise.

And after a few hours, it begins to work on his mind. I mean, when you're trying to maintain a state of readiness and alertness, you tend to respond to every little sound. And after doing that for a couple of hours, something happens to your state of readiness and alertness.

For one thing, you begin to feel drowsy. Sleepy, Stuporous. Comatose. Even if you've had a nice long nap.

It must have been sometime past midnight when I realized that I was in danger of falling asleep. One of the things you can do to stay awake on a stake-out is talk to your partner. I decided to give it a shot.

"Drover, it's time to check in. Have you seen any*zzzzzzz* . . .?"

"No thanks, I couldn't hold another bite *zzzzzzzzz*."

"Uh, Roger, did you *zzzzzzz* get a count on 'em?"

"Three green elephants dancing with a . . . zzzzzz."

"Come back on that one, Roger, we didn't have a good . . . zzzzzz"

"Oh yeah, I've been wide asleep for . . . steak bones."

"Right. Well, I'm having a little troub . . . Beulah, you shouldn't be here at this hour of the . . . having a little trouble staying . . . asleep myzzzzzzzzzelf. How about you?"

"Oh sure, I'll take all three . . . . snort zzzzzz."

"Check and double zzzzz . . . got to stay asleep, no matter how hard it . . . zzzzzzz.

"Fiddle music."

"You bet. And the fiddler it is, the musicker I like it."

"Pete, I hear fiddle . . . fiddle-faddle . . . fiddle music."

"Don't be obserd, Droving. Pete can't play a . . . what did you say?"

"Who?"

"Just now. Someone was talking about Pete."

"No, that must have been . . . fiddle music."

"You keep talking about . . . fiddle musle . . . zzzzz."

"I keep hearing . . . middle fusic . . . and steak bones."

"It's just the crickles, Droving. Crickets."

"Do crickles play . . . fickle music?"

"Roger, a big ten-four on the crickles."

Crickle? Fickle? Fiddle?

HUH?

Fiddle! Hey, unless my ears were deceiving me, I was hearing FIDDLE MUSIC! But that was impossible. Nobody on my ranch played the . . . nobody on my ranch had ever played the . . .

I sat up and gave my head a shake. Just for a second there, I must have dozed off for a second or two. Not long, just a momentary lapse of a split second or two, but long enough to . . .

Drover was dead asleep, the little dunce, sleeping on the job, sleeping through a very important stake-out, and I had a good mind to . . .

That WAS fiddle music, and I wasn't dreaming it. Not that I had been asleep, you understand, or that I might have been dreaming about anything at all, but on the other hand . . . .

I took my ears off Automatic Liftup and switched over to manual. I raised them to the

G.L.Holmes

Full Alert position, trimmed them out to Max G (that's our shorthand term for "Maximum Gathering Mode," don't you see), and homed in on the alleged sound frequency.

Fiddle music. No question about it. I could hear it as plain as day, but still my mind refused to accept it as real. And yet . . . I had picked it up on Max G, so it had to be the real thing.

Very carefully, I threaded my nose through the weeds in front of me, pushing them aside so as to give myself a clear and unobsconded view of the chicken house. Everything appeared to be normal, but then . . . .

HOLY SMOKES!!

My tail stuck straight out and the hair on my back shot straight up and my ears jumped three inches and cold chills went rolling down my backbone.

I blinked my eyes, trying to convince them that they had malfunctioned. No luck there. Hence, after running checks and double-checks on all my sensory equipment, I still saw . . . *a fox playing a fiddle, and strolling towards the chicken house.*

I saw it, fellers, and I heard it, but I still didn't believe it. I had a peculiar reaction to this situation. I turned away and looked the other direction, hoping to give my racing mind a chance to catch up with . . . I'm not sure what a racing mind would catch up with, but the point is that I needed a moment to absorb all this.

I tried to think and pull together bits of evidence and testimony and clues that I had gathered over the past several days. Chicken house. Broken eggs. J. T. Cluck's bizarre story about hearing fiddle music in the night. Drover's unbelievable tale about a fox playing a fiddle, which he himself had dismissed as nothing but a dream.

But perhaps Drover had been mistaken. Perhaps he had misled me, thrown me off the trail, just as he had done so many times over the years. For you see, it was beginning to appear that the fox playing fiddle was NOT a dream at all, but an actual reality.

And the most astounding thing of all was that I had suspected it all along.

Yes, it was all coming back now and the pieces of the puzzle began falling into place. I took a deep breath and turned my eyes back to the chicken house, ready now to resume my observation.

It was a fox, all right. In his original testimony, Drover had noted, and this is a direct quote, "We don't have foxes around here." Almost true but not quite. We don't have red foxes or gray foxes or your other varieties of northern foxes, but we do have a few kit foxes.

Your kit fox is about half the size of a coyote, don't you see, which makes him a fairly small animal. He has a long pointed nose, beady little eyes, a light red coat, and a bushy tail. He lives in holes and eats such items as mice, grasshoppers, and rabbits.

Or, when he can get them, he loves to eat anything he might find in a chicken house.

They're bad about thieving, them foxes, but very few of them play fiddles. This one was a little out of the ordinary in that respect.

So what we had going on at that moment was a kit fox, walking slowly towards the chicken house and playing a tune on a fiddle, which pretty muchly fit into the pattern I had worked up earlier that day.

The question now was, should I come out of hiding and use the Riot Axe on this little villain, or should I remain hidden and see what he would do?

Since I didn't actually have an air-tight case against him, I decided to go with Opinion Two. I would remain hidden in the weeds, observe his every movement and gesture, and then, if he made one false move, I would spring my deadly trap on him.

And I really had suspected a fox all along. Honest.

CHAPTER

7

FIDDLE HYPNOSIS, AND HOW I MANAGED TO RESIST IT

Okay. So there I was, and here's what I saw.

This fox came strolling down the gravel drive, the one that lays between the machine shed and the chicken house. The moon was bright enough so that I got a good look at him.

I've already given a partial description, but I'll do it again: kind of small and wiry, light red coat of hair, sharp pointed nose, cunning little eyes, long bushy tail with a splash of white on the tip end.

He had that fiddle tucked under his chin and he was playing this tune and kind of singing along with it: "Dee dee dee-dum, dee dee dee dum-dee-dum dee dee, dee dee dee dee dee dum, dum dee dum dee dee dee dee.''

And smiling. Did I mention that? Yes sir, had his eyes closed and he was smiling to himself, just as though he didn't have a care in the world and was doing exactly what he ought to be doing.

Now, I have to admit that after I'd watched and listened for a minute or two, the hair on my back began to lay down and the cold chills stopped skating down my spine. After I got over the initial shock of seeing a fox playing a fiddle in the dead of night, I sort of settled back and, well, enjoyed the music, you might say.

It wasn't half bad. In fact, it was pretty good. That little fox had obviously taken a lesson or two on the fiddle, and he was making some derned fine music—and I consider myself a pretty severe critic of such things.

And the longer I watched and listened, the more I found myself hoping that he wouldn't go into the chicken house. I mean, I've got no grudge against foxes. As long as they stay away from headquarters and leave my chickens alone, I've got no quarrel with them whatsoever.

On the other hand, any creature that goes where he shouldn't on my outfit becomes my mortal enemy. Whether he's a fox or a coyote or a coon or a Bengal tiger, it's all the same to me. He gets persecuted to the fullest extent of the law.

Well, for a while there, it appeared that he would be content to play for himself in the moonlight, and as I say, I was kind of enjoying the concert. That was a snappy little tune he was playing, the kind that makes you want to tap your paw.

And as a matter of fact, I did catch myself tapping my paw a time or two. Not anything serious, just a little tap here and there.

But then . . . I raised up and lifted my ears and narrowed my eyes. Was he drifting closer to the chicken house? Yes, he definitely appeared to be drifting towards the little door in the middle of the chicken house.

That was too bad. The scene to come flashed across my mind. The fox would stop playing, cast cunning and greedy glances to the left and to the right, and dive through the opening.

This would be followed at once by an explosion of squawking and a blizzard of feathers as terrified chickens came flapping out the little door. A moment later, the villain would appear again, with egg all over his face and a murdered hen clenched in his jaws.

And at that point, I would have no choice but to emerge from my hiding place in the weeds, bark an alarm to the house, and lumber down to settle all accounts with the villain.

And his life would end there in front of the chicken house he had just robbed, snuffed out like a candle, either by the Head of Ranch Security or by a blast from Loper's shotgun.

And he would take his music with him to the grave. No more would we hear his fiddle in the moonlight.

It would be a sad and sorry ending, and I would have much preferred a better one. But when you're Head of Ranch Security, you have to write the endings as they come, and some of 'em ain't real happy.

I pushed myself up and tried to steel my iron will for what was about to come. The moment I heard the first chicken squawk, I would have to push the Button of No Return, for you see, if a chicken squawked and I didn't sound the alarm, my boss would have grounds for stripping me of my rank and position.

And dog food.

Oh, terrible decision! Oh, heavy burden of

responsibility! I hoped against hope that the fox wouldn't dart inside and that no chicken would . . . .

Hmmm. That was odd. The fox DIDN'T dart inside and no chicken DID squawk.

Now, this was stretching my powers of credulation. By George, I couldn't believe what I was . . . two hens appeared at the door, and unless my eyes were playing tricks on me, *they invited the fox inside!*

Hence, there was no squawking or flapping of wings, no signs of a forced entry. Hence, how could I . . . hmmm. Was it against Ranch Law for a fox to be INVITED into the chicken house?

Ordinarily, my mind moves very quickly over matters of law and crinimality, and comes up with solutions in a matter of seconds. But this deal had me stumped.

If a fox in the chicken house wasn't a problem for the chickens, then maybe it shouldn't be a problem for the Head of Ranch Security, is sort of the way I framed it up. So why should I risk my life and limb protecting a bunch of dumb chickens who didn't appear to think they needed protecting?

Okay. The fox stopped playing, smiled at the chickens, and gave them a little bow. And

G.L. Holmes

then he said, "Uh, good evening, ladies. Shall I come in and play a few tunes on my fiddle?"

They motioned him inside. He threw a glance over his shoulder and hopped through the little door.

"Drover," I whispered, "this beats anything I ever saw. Cover me. I'm going down there to have a look."

"Morgle gurgle skiffering steak bones."

I pushed myself up, slipped out of the weeds, and began stalking towards the chicken house, taking one cautious step at a time. After covering a short distance in Stealthy Crouch Mode, I switched over to a faster pace and sprinted the rest of the way.

Upon reaching the chicken house, I flattened myself against the front of the building and peered through the opening—and witnessed a very strange sight.

The fox stood right in the middle of things, playing a song on his fiddle and showing that same contented smile I had seen before. And get this. All around him, the chickens were . . . you ain't going to believe this, but here goes . . . the chickens were dancing the Panhandle Two-step!

There was J. T. Cluck squiring some old hen around near the east wall, perhaps the same

Elsa we had heard so much about. The rest of the couples were hens, dancing together. And they seemed no more concerned about the fox in the midst than if he'd been a fly or another chicken.

But here's the clinker. While the hens were dancing, that fox would lean over, stick his sharp nose into a nest, gobble an egg, and spit out the shells—and never miss a beat on that fiddle.

He did all this in full view of the chickens, and it didn't cause one ripple of concern.

So! Now I understood why we hadn't heard squawks of alarm the night before. It was an inside job! In giving me his testimony, J. T. Cluck had either lied to cover up his part in the conspiracy or . . . or else, for reasons I couldn't explain, he'd had no memory of the event.

Yes indeed, the wheels were turning now. I had pretty muchly firmed up my case and now the time had come for me to bust in there and . . . .

Sure was pretty music, the sweetest fiddle you ever heard. If there's one thing this old world's short on, it's sweet fiddle music. I couldn't remember when I'd . . . .

I could almost understand how a bunch of

chickens might invite this guy into their house and . . . what else did a chicken have to do with its time? And it seemed fairly reasonable that they might pay him off in eggs, didn't it? What else could . . . .

You know, there's something almost hypnotic about a fid . . . flowers and pretty girls and young love, and me and Beulah . . . one-two-three-four, one-two-three-four . . . dancing around the room, her big collie eyes . . . something almost hypnotic about fiddle music.

I mean, a guy has to concentrate real hard on his . . . one-two-three-four, a one-two-three-four . . . sweetest fiddle . . . on his business or he could very easily get . . . "Oh Hank, you're a wonderful dancer!" . . . one-two-three-four, one-two-three-four . . . "Beulah, you've never been more beautiful than you are tonight" ". . . Hank, how did you know that I love fiddle music?"

Anyway, the point is that if a guy didn't concentrate pretty hard on his fiddle, he could sure get caught up in that sweet business music, because there's something hypnotic . . . .

Pink streaks of dawn on the eastern horizon? That was odd. I must have dozed . . . I sat up and blinked my eyes. The music had stopped and the chicken house was dark and quiet.

Somehow the night had slipped away from me, and perhaps that sneaking, egg-stealing fox had slipped away with it, which kind of annoyed me, don't you know, seeing as how I'd intended to . . . .

Ah ha and oh ho! He hadn't slipped away from me, because at that very moment I saw his bushy tail appear at the door, as he came backing out.

I leaped to my feet and puffed myself up to my full height and massiveness, and announced to one startled fox, "Freeze, turkey! You're under arrest!"

CHAPTER

8

FRANKIE THE FOX

Yes sir, that was one startled fox!

Oh, he'd thought he was so clever, so slick, so smooth, thought he'd hipnopottomized me along with a bunch of silly chickens, thought he'd pulled his deal off without a hitch, and now that the sun was coming up, he figgered he'd just slip away and nobody would be any the wiser.

But what he hadn't counted on was running into the Head of Ranch Security, and when you don't count on that, fellers, you might as well not bother to count.

I had caught him red-handed and red-faced and . . . well, he was basically red, see, but nevertheless I had caught him climbing out of the chicken house, which was just about enough evidence to get a guy shot by an angry cowboy.

Well, when I gave him the "Freeze, turkey, you're under arrest!" treatment, his head shot up and he raised his front paws, one of which held the fiddle and the other of which held the bow. He stood motionless while I stepped over and frixed him. Fricksed him. Frisked him.

"Okay, now turn around real slow and keep those paws up there where I can see 'em." He turned around, and I could see that I had struck terror in his heart—which was no accident. "All right, let's start with your name."

"Huhhie huh huh," he said.

"Say that again. I missed part of it." He said it again, and once again I heard only sounds which meant nothing. I was about to lose patience and get tough with him when he pointed the fiddle bow at his mouth and . . . oh, yes, he had . . . .

"I see you have an egg in your mouth, Foxie, which not only establishes your guilt beyond a doubt but also makes it impossible for you to give me your name. Lay the egg down and state your name. And don't try any funny stuff."

He set the egg down on the ground between us and gave me a friendly smile. "They call me Frankie the Fox, and could you tell me where I might find the head guard dog of this fine ranch?"

"Frankie the Fox, huh? Well, you've out-foxed yourself this time because you happen to be talking with none other than Hank the Cowdog, Head of Ranch Security."

"Oh good! Hank, I looked and looked for you when I came by here earlier in the evening, wanted to check in and make sure everything was copesetic, 'cause if there's anything Frankie the Fox does not want to do, it's get off on the wrong foot with the guy in charge."

He gave me a wink and a grin.

"Yeah, well, you've found the guy in charge, all right."

"I can see that! You just look like somebody who's got things under control."

"A lot of people say that, so I guess there must be some truth to it. I didn't know it was so obvious."

"Uh Hank, it is obvious! It is, it really is. You have that certain special look about you." He stepped back and squinted one eye and gave me a thorough looking-over. "Oh yes, very definitely. Out of all the dogs in Ochiltree County, I would have picked YOU out as the Head of Ranch Security.''

''I'll be derned, that's pretty impressive, and I'm glad to know . . . . On the other hand, we mustn't forget that I've just caught you in the act of slipping out of the chicken house.''

''Oh that! Don't think a thing about that, son. I was glad to do it. If this fiddle of mine can make them old gals laugh and dance—why, Hank, life has no greater reward than that!''

''Yes, well I . . . .''

''And I'll tell you this.'' He tapped me on the shoulder with his bow. ''I'm just a poor old fox, I've got nothing to show for my years on this earth but a broke-down fiddle and a five-hair bow, but son, I have had the high honor of bringing pleasure and joy into the lives of others.''

I cleared my throat. ''Yes. That's wonderful.''

''It is, believe me.''

''But there's still this little matter of the eggs.''

''Hank, what I'm a-fixing to say comes from the bottom of my heart, and I want you to listen.'' He looked me square in the eyes.

"Them eggs wouldn't mean any more to me if they were made of solid gold. Please, please don't be embarrassed."

"Well, actually I . . . ."

"It was the best you could do. It was the best the chickens could do. And that's good enough for Frankie the Fox. If the day ever comes when Frankie won't play his fiddle for a few eggs, son, may I be struck dead by uh—lightning!"

Somehow this wasn't . . . . "The point is, I caught you in the act of stealing eggs, and on this outfit, stealing eggs is a pretty serious crime."

He narrowed his eyes and the smile fell away from his mouth. "Stealing eggs? You think I was *a-stealing eggs*"?

"That's correct."

He came over and put a paw around my shoulder. "Hank. Hank, son! Let me explain something to you. You are a smart dog, but you have been on this ranch too long. It has done something to your mind. You are a-getting too serious about things.

"Now look here. If I had been a common thief, do you think them hens would have invited me in? And if I had been a-stealin' their eggs, don't you reckon they would have made some noise about it? Now, search your heart, Hank, and tell the truth.''

''Yes, well I did . . . wonder about that . . . a little.''

''Of course you did! Your mind said I was a-stealing eggs, but your heart said, ''No. He ain't a-stealing eggs. He's a-making our hens happy, and tomorrow they'll lay more eggs than ever.' ''

He stepped back and gave me kind of a sad smile. ''Here I am, Hank, I'm just a poor old fox who tries to get by and make the world a little brighter. If you think the world would be a better place if I was called a common thief and punished for it, then go ahead and do it. I ain't a-going to run. And if your heart tells you that I should be shot, I'll even leave you my fiddle.''

Well, that made me feel like a louse, him offering to . . . it would have been much easier for me to turn him in if he'd acted like a thief and run away. But he didn't.

Hey, this was a tough decision. My mind said he was a-stealing eggs, but my heart said, ''No. He wasn't a-stealin eggs. He was a-making our hens happy, and tomorrow they'll lay more eggs than ever.''

And he *was* an extra fine fiddle player, which was no small bananas.

By this time the lights had come on down at the house. It would be easy to sound the alarm and bring Loper to the scene with his gun.

I paced back and forth, wrestling with this decision, trying to sort out what was right and what was wrong. After several long heart-pounding minutes, I stopped pacing.

"Okay, I've reached a decision."

"Good. And Hank, I want you to know that whichever way it goes, we're still friends."

"I've decided, after much soul-searching and deliberizing, to let it slide—this time."

Frankie the Fox grinned and gave me a little bow. "You're a very wise dog. I'd take my hat off to you, Hank, but you know, I'm just a poor old fox and I never could afford . . . ."

"Never mind the sad story. I'll let it slide this time, but you've got to promise to stay away from my chicken house. Whether it's stealing or not, you're making me look bad."

A look of pain came over his face. "Hank, son! I would never, ever do anything that made you look bad. Believe me."

"Then you'll stay away from my outfit. Oh, and one more thing. I'm going to put this last egg back where it belongs. It just doesn't look right for you to be walking away with an egg."

"Hank, if that's what your old heart tells you to do, then that's what you should do."

I gave him a sour look. "I'd feel better about this whole deal if you'd quit talking about my heart. Somehow that makes me uneasy."

I scooped the egg up in my powerful jaws and slipped through the door. I was in the process of looking for a nest in which to deposit the egg when . . . .

I never had much respect for the intelligence of a chicken. Some animals, such as cats, are merely dumb. Chickens are dumb dumb. Do you think those chickens were glad to see their Head of Ranch Security? Do you suppose they showed me any gratitude or gave me any praise for staying up all night to protect their stupid . . . ?

No. Here's what they did. I nuzzled a sleeping hen with my nose, see, with the idea of dropping the egg into her nest. Her eyes popped open, her beak popped open, and she began shrieking and flapping her wings.

"IT'S A FOX, IT'S A FOX!!" she screamed. Well, that woke up the whole house, and within seconds, every bird in the place was screaming, "It's a fox, it's a fox!"

G.L. Holmes

Dumb birds.

Furthermore, she smacked me across the nose with one of her stupid flapping wings and . . . all at once I felt a pleasant warm sensation spreading across the interior portion of my mouth and . . . I'd never supposed that I would go for the taste of . . . I mean, eating raw eggs was sort of a violation of the law in our part of the . . . .

Hmmmmm. Not bad. In fact, all at once I could kind of understand how a guy might . . . I spit out the shells and peered into the nest and saw . . . hmmmmmmmmmmm.

It seemed to me that I was entitled to *something* for all my hard work and sacrifice. I mean, I'd been up all night guarding the chicken house, right? And a little old measly egg was the only payment they could come up with.

I, uh, accepted their offer, so to speak. It would have been tacky to turn it down . . . don't you see.

But in the meantime, that chicken house had turned into a bee hive, with birds flying around in all directions, feathers floating through the air, chickens bouncing off the walls, squawking, flapping, and it was then that I heard the back door slam down at the . . . .

HUH?

I was, well, sort of in the chicken house. With several eggs' worth of evidence on my face. And the chickens were making a terrible racket. And this appeared to be one of those situations that could lead to a misunderstanding.

Which is basically why I decided to get the heck out of there.

I shot through the door and scrambled outside. There was Frankie, shaking his head and scowling. "Son, you have a heavy touch with the chickens. I don't know what your plans are right now, but old Frankie is a-fixin' to shuffle along."

"Yes, and I think I'll walk you to the county road or thereabouts."

We were streaking away from the chicken house, and just as we got underway, we met Drover coming out of the machine shed.

"Hank, I heard . . . a fox . . . egg on your face . . . what . . . oh, my gosh, Hank, what's going on here?

"Never mind, Drover. Either run for your life or prepare to answer some tough questions when Loper gets here!"

"Oh my gosh! I think I'll run, if this old leg . . . ."

With Frankie in the lead, we swooped around the west side of the machine shed and took aim for the cap rocks to the north. I was hoping with all my heart and mind and soul that Loper wouldn't see us running away, since that might have raised troublesome questions about our participation, so to speak, in the chicken house incident.

When I heard the gun go off and heard the buckshot whistling overhead, my heart sank. After years of loyal service to the ranch, my career as Head of Ranch Security had come to a sudden end. Just like that: in the snap of a finger, in the blink of an eye. All gone.

And all over a little misunderstanding.

CHAPTER

9

THE FAMOUS FRANKIE AND HANKIE CHICKEN HOUSE BAND

We didn't slow down until we reached a deep ravine at the base of that big cap rock north of headquarters. There, we took cover and caught our breath.

After a short rest, I turned to the fox. "Frankie, I'm not much inclined to jump to hasty conclusions, but I have a feeling that we might have worn out our welcome at the ranch."

His brows lifted. "Uh yes, I think it would be safe to say that."

"In which case it might follow from simple logic that I have just, so to speak, taken early retirement from my position as Head of Ranch Security."

"Yes, that might follow, sure might."

"In which case," I began pacing back and forth in front of him, "in which case, as unfair and unjust as that might be, it also follows from simple logic that I am 'unemployed,' you might say. Or, to put it another way, cast out of my job and home."

"Uh huh, yes."

I stopped pacing. "Shall I go straight to the point, Frankie?"

"Well, son, since I don't know what the point is, I can't help you much there."

"All right, okay, fine. I'll go straight to the point. I'm out of a job, Frankie. I'm in a bind. What are the chances that I could throw in with you and become a traveling musician? I have a heck of a fine voice—that is, people tell me that all the time—and I play a little banjo."

He looked at me with narrowed eyes. "Can you read any music?"

"Uh . . . no."

"Have you ever had lessons?"

"Well . . . not exactly lessons, but let me hasten to say . . . ."

He raised his paw and smiled. "Son, it sounds to me like you'd fit right into my deal, and in a word, yes, I'd be glad to have you."

For a moment there, I couldn't believe my oars. Ears.

"Really? You mean that? Holy smokes, what a piece of luck! I can see it now: our names up in lights, wimmen coming from all around to hear the Famous Frankie and Hankie Chicken House Band! It's a dream come true, Frankie. This could turn out to be one of the best days of . . . ."

At that moment, Drover interrupted me and called me aside for a private conference. "Hank, who is that guy, and how come we ran away from the ranch, and what are we doing here?"

"Oh, yes. I almost forgot." I briefed him on the events that had led up to our sudden departure from the ranch.

"So, as you can see, Drover, Frankie was merely entertaining our chickens, and I was merely returning the egg to its proper nesting place. Everything would have turned out fine if the stupid chickens had kept their traps shut."

Drover glanced at me, then at Frankie. "But Hank, he's the fox! And he was *eating eggs*. That's what we were guarding against."

"I've already explained that, Drover. The

91

eggs were a gift from the chickens."

"But *you* were eating eggs too. I know, because you've got egg all over your mouth."

I swept a paw over my mouth and turned away. "That's, uh, your interpretation of what you think you see on my mouth, Drover, and I'd caution you about leaping to conclusions."

"You were eating eggs and that fox was eating eggs, and oh my gosh, what am I doing here with two egg-robbers!"

He started crying. I waited until the tears had stopped dripping off his chin.

"Drover, there's a down-side and an up-side to all of life's experiences. The down-side here is that, yes, we have been ruined, our reputations are destroyed, we've lost our ranch, and we have now joined the crinimal element of society."

"Ohhhhhh!"

"On the up-side, we've got an opportunity to join Frankie's band and become traveling musicians."

"Musicians! I can't even carry a tune!"

"Yes, I'm aware of that, Drover, but we mustn't let a mere lack of talent stand in our way. Perhaps we can start you out on washtub bass."

"I don't want to play washtub bass. I don't want to be a traveling musician. I want to go home!"

"You're being hysterical."

"I'm being honest!"

"All right, you're being hysterically honest, but that's nothing to get hysterical about."

"Hank, I want to go home."

I glared at the runt. "How could you possibly choose to go back to the ranch? What does it have that you couldn't find in greater abundance out here in the wild, as a free dog and a traveling musician?"

"Food. I'm starting to wonder where my next meal's going to come from."

"Next meal! Drover, how can you . . . ?" That was an interesting point, come to think of it, where we would find our next meal now that we'd been dispossessed and turned out into the world. "Drover, I'm sure . . . what do you think of that, Frankie? I mean, just for the sake of argument. And by the way, Frankie, this is Drover. Drover, meet Frankie the Fox."

Frankie smiled and tuned on his fiddle. "Boys, let me tell you. Old Frankie has been a-living off the land for a long time, and it ain't failed him yet." He arched his brows. "There's several chicken houses in this valley. I know, because I've played in all of 'em at one time or another, and they do provide.''

"There's your answer, Drover. You've got nothing to worry about.''

He placed a paw over his eyes. "Except maybe getting shot for stealing eggs. And I don't even like raw eggs.''

"Drover, every line of work has its little . . . .'' I turned back to the fox. "Any chance

G. L. Holmes

94

we might, uh, get shot or something like that?"

"Oh sure. It goes with the territory. I've been a-dodgin' buckshot all my life, and I'll admit there's a couple of BB's in my hind end that I didn't get out of the way of quick enough. But son, bein' a musician ain't an easy life."

"I see. Yes. Well, if there's any way we could, uh, cut down on the shooting aspect . . . some of us enjoy that brand of adventure more than others, shall we say, and while I've always toyed with the idea of becoming a traveling musician, I've never toyed with the idea of becoming shot."

Drover let out a wail. "I don't want to get shot! I want to be a good dog and go home to my old gunny sack bed."

"Son," said the fox, "your belly will answer a lot of them philosophical questions for you, and it won't take long. Now, I'm going to move along down the creek. I know a nice little chicken house down there, and I ain't played it for a while. Y'all can do as you wish."

"That's good enough for me," I said. "Come on, Drover, here's your chance to quit a lousy ranch job and strike out on a new adventure.''

Frankie and I headed east in a trot, but Drover didn't move. I stopped and yelled back at him. ''Well, what are you waiting for? Come on.''

''I just can't do it, Hank.''

''Fine. Go on back to the ranch, be a chicken-liver and see if anybody cares. While you're sleeping your life away under the gas tanks, I'll be out in the wide and wonderful world, making music, charming the wimmen, signing autographs, and feasting on the applause of the multitudes.''

He started slinking towards the ranch. ''Yeah, I know I'll be missing out on all the adventure.''

''You certainly will, but you're old enough to make your own decisions now, and the fact that you've just made one of the dumbest decisions in history isn't important.''

''Thanks, Hank. Bye. I'll miss you.''

''Yes, and I'll . . . goodbye, Drover, you little dunce. I hope . . . goodbye!''

And with that, I turned my back on Drover and on the ranch I had loved and worked for so many years, and went plunging into a new career as an outlaw and musician.

It was late afternoon when Frankie and I reached the spot, just below Slim's cowboy shack, where Wolf Creek and Cottonwood Creek come together. We stopped there for a little rest.

This was all familiar country to me. I'd explored it several times before, while on my way to pay visits to the One Love of My Life, the world's most gorgious collie dog, the lovely Miss . . . .

Hmmm.

I hadn't bothered to ask Frankie the Fox exactly where we were going, and I seemed to recall that there was a chicken house on Beulah's . . . hmmmmmmm.

I wandered over to where Frankie was sitting, under a high bluff where he was fiddling around with his fiddle.

"Say, Frankie, where'd you say that chicken house was?"

He pointed his bow to the east and gave me a wink. "Next ranch down the creek. All we have to do is wait for, uh, darkness to fall."

Hmmmmmmmmm.

You know, it had been quite a spell since I'd seen that woman. She'd been on my mind just about every day and night, but shucks, I'd been so tied down with investigations and murders and monster reports . . . .

I moved a little closer to the fox. "Frankie, your fiddle music seems to work miracles on lady chickens. You ever notice that it's had a special effect on . . . well, just to pull an example out of the hat . . . on *lady dogs*?"

He grinned. "It's a funny thing about this old fiddle. The ladies do, uh, kind of like it." He winked.

"Yes, that's what I . . . that's very interesting." I paced back and forth in front of him. "Frankie, there's this collie gal who stays on the very ranch we're going to, and I've been trying to strike sparks with her for a long time, don't you see, and . . . Frankie, I've got a small favor to ask."

"Oh?"

"I want you to listen to this song."

CHAPTER
10
A CLEVER PLAN TO SWEEP MISS BEULAH OFF HER FEET

My Heart Is Up For Rent

Now Frank, Miss Beulah, my amor,
That collie gal that I adore,
Has managed to escape my snares and
   traps.
I know it doesn't make much sense,
That she's resisted such a prince,
But she derned sure has, and that is just
   a fact.

I've gone to visit her at night,
Howled at the moon, got into fights,
And once I even tried rolling on a
   skunk.

That coyote trick didn't hardly work,
She's still in love with that same old jerk
Named Plato, and my hopes are pret'
   near sunk.

   Oh, my heart is up for rent,
   My love's been living in a tent.
   I struck a spark and built a fire.
   And got the heartburn of desire.

This game of love is pretty rough,
I've had this heartburn long enough.
But what the heck's a dog supposed to
   do?
You chase the girls, they run away,
But if you quit, they want to play.
Who wrote these dadgum rules, I'm ask-
   ing you?

Miss Beulah's tough as nails, I fear,
The hardest case of my career,
I just don't understand what makes her
   tick.

Now, surely, Frank, there's ways and
   means
Of working me into her dreams.
It's time for me to find a magic trick.

Oh, my heart is up for rent,
My love's been living in a tent.
I struck a spark and built a fire.
And got the heartburn of desire.

Well Hank, it happens that you've found
A fiddlin' fox who's been around
And knows a thing or two 'bout charm-
    ing gals.
See, all I do to turn it on
Is tell this fiddle to play a song,
And soon I have 'em standin' in my
    corrals.

So if that heartburn's got you down,
And if you're tired of being a clown,
Just give old Frankie the Fox your shop-
    ping list.
I'll play a jig, I'll play a song,
She'll think she was hit by an atom
    bomb,
I tell you, son, this fiddle has never
    missed.

Oh, my heart is up for rent,
My love's been living in a tent.
I struck a spark and built a fire.
And got the heartburn of desire.

I'll play a jig, I'll call a dance,
That collie gal won't have a chance.
That empty heart will soon be occupied,
    brother.
That empty heart will soon be occupied.

When we were done with the song, Frankie turned to me and smiled. "Say no more. It will be done."

And you know what? In three minutes' time, me and that fox had worked out a plan that was guaranteed to sweep the lovely Miss Beulah off her feet, into my awaiting arms, and out of the clutches of Plato the bird dog.

Have I mentioned Plato before? Yes, of course I have. Plato had been a thorn in my paw for a long time, the problem being that, for reasons I had never understood, Beulah had some silly attachment to the mutt.

How any woman in her right mind could choose a bird dog over . . . but let's don't get started on that. The point is that for years and years I had searched for the magic formula, the secret love potion, the short cut to her heart, only to be turned away and disappointed. Crushed, actually.

Devastated.

Destroyed.

Left sitting in the ruins of a love story.

Completely wrecked emotionally, hardly able to eat or drink or carry on my work.

Just, by George, wiped out.

On the other hand, I had never had a fiddle-playing fox working for me. If he could charm eggs out of a bunch of hens, there was a real good chance that . . . heh. It hardly seemed fair, but who wants to be fair anyway?

We didn't wait for darkness to fall, but set out right away for Beulah's place. Did I feel good? No sir, I felt absolutely splendifferous!

We followed the creek until we came to that section of dense willows that lies just below the house. Then we turned south and proceeded in a . . . well, a southerly direction, of course.

As planned, Frankie took cover behind a big native elm on the north edge of the yard, and I went on. I hadn't gone far when I came upon The Bird Dog.

He was practicing his pointing routines—creeping up on an old tennis shoe and then freezing, with his nose and tail sticking straight out at opposite ends of his body, and one foot poised in the air.

As you may know, bird dogs get very serious about such things as tennis shoes and old socks, and Plato was so absorbed in bird-dogging his tennis shoe that he didn't hear me creeping up behind him.

And I, being something of a prankster, couldn't resist giving him a little shock. At the same moment, I yelled, "Dog-eating tennis shoe!" And gave him a good swat on the behind.

G. L. Holmes

"AAAAAA-EEEEEE!"

Ho ho, his little pointing routine fell apart—
hee, hee—as he flew straight up in the—ha,
ha—air, I loved it. He had run a good 10 yards
before he figgered out that he hadn't been attacked by a dog-eating tennis shoe. At that
point, he stopped and came back, looking a little embarrassed.

"Well, by golly, you gave me quite a scare!
Good old Hank, always good for a laugh.
Hank, you won't believe this, but just this very
morning, I said to Beulah, I said, 'Honey-lamb,
I wonder what's happened to our old friend
Hank.' "

"Honey-lamb?"

"That's Beulah, that's what I call her, and
she calls me Sugarbun. It probably sounds
silly."

"Yeah, probably does."

"But Hank, we're just as happy as a couple
of larks down here, couldn't be better, every
little thing is just wonderful!"

"That's wonderful."

"Isn't it though? That's what I tell Beulah,
and oh, I'll bet you want to see her. Honey-
lamb!" He called her and then gave me a wink.
"She'll be SO surprised to see you here, and
I'm SO happy for her! You two get together

and talk about old times, Hank, and I'll go on and finish my workout, and then we'll all get together and talk and laugh and just have a wonderful time."

"You bet."

"Make yourself at home, Hank. What's mine is yours."

"Yes, I know."

He went on with his workout, never dreaming what schemes were bubbling in my mind.

I hid behind a little bush and watched her coming down from the front porch: the fine collie nose, the flaxen hair, the deep brown eyes, the ears that flapped in the breeze.

Mercy! Any dog would gladly give his life for such a woman. Fortunately, I had come up with a better plan.

"Plato? Plato, did you call?" She still hadn't seen me. About 10 feet away, she stopped and looked around.

I stepped from the bush, and in a voice as thick and sweet as sorghum molasses, I said, "Hello, Beulah."

I saw the startled look come into her eyes as old memories came rushing to the surface. She was startled, puzzled, bewildered, and then torn between the true love she'd always felt for me and the false, counterfeit, shabby emotions she felt for Plato.

Yes, I could see it all passing across her face in the space of a few seconds. Finally she spoke. "Why . . . Hank! What are you doing here?"

I gave her a secret smile. "I think you know, Beulah."

"No, I really don't. "

"Of course you do. I've come to save you."

"Save . . . me? Save me from what?"

"You know, Beulah, and I know that you know, and you know that I know that you know, and there's no sense in pretending."

"Oh Hank, I hope you're not still thinking about . . . us."

I laughed and immediately switched to Plan B. "Oh no. No. No, no. I have my life and you have yours."

She sighed and began to relax, heh heh. "That's right, Hank, and I'm glad."

"You have your life, Beulah, and I have mine, and we've gone our separate ways."

"But we can still be friends."

"Exactly. Yes, the best of friends who can talk and laugh and share secret thoughts."

"I've always enjoyed talking to you, Hank.

You're a very interesting dog, and in many ways . . . well, we mustn't stir the waters."

"No indeed, Beulah. It wouldn't be fair to either of us because, after all, we have our own lives and that's the way it ought to be. Why, if one of us didn't have a life . . . there would be only one of us left, I guess you'd say, and that would be no fun at all."

"Oh Hank," she laughed, and hey, I could see that old sparkle in her eyes, "you have such a funny way of saying things."

"Yes indeed, my sweet darling, uh, friend . . . friend of many years and shared experiences, and why don't we take a little walk down by that big native elm tree? It's a beautiful tree, don't you think?"

I began easing her towards the tree.

"Well, yes, I suppose it is."

"Gorgious tree. I've always admired that tree. You know, Beulah, the problem with dogs today is that they don't take the time to appreciate the beauty of trees."

She laughed again. "Is that the problem with dogs today? I had wondered."

"Yes indeed, just move along, my dear, that's better, just a few more steps and, bingo, here we are."

We had reached the base of the tree, on the

other side of which lurked my secret musical weapon.

"Well," she said, taking a deep breath of fragrant air, "it is a very nice tree. What shall we talk about?"

"Oh, I don't know, why don't we talk about fiddle music?"

"Fiddle music?"

"Sure, why not? For years we've never talked about fiddle music. Tell me, my, uh, friend, my good friend, what do you think of fiddle music?"

For a moment she ducked her head. Then her big dewy eyes came up and she smiled. "I suppose you already know that I just LOVE fiddle music, but I'm sorry to say that I never get to hear enough of it."

Ho boy, was this deal working? Old Hank had set the trap of love, and now he was fixing to release the spring.

CHAPTER

11

THE TRAP OF LOVE BACKFIRES

"Beulah, my prairie winecup, I can't say that I knew that you loved fiddle music, but I did sort of suspect it. Now, if you will close your eyes, I will produce from the ectoplasmic vapors of the atmosphere some of the most gorgious fiddle music you have ever heard."

She twisted her head and gave me a puzzled look. "Are you joking? How can you . . . ?"

"Never mind the questions, my little sunflower. Close your eyes, open your ears, and hang on to your heart. Ready? Here we go!"

Good old Frankie the Fox! He came in right on cue and played a real pretty little number. I watched my prey . . . uh, my darling as she swayed back and forth with the pure sweet sounds of the fiddle. I could see that she was becoming vulnerable and more vulnerable all the time.

"Beulah, may I have the honor of this dance?"

"Oh, I shouldn't . . . but . . . maybe just one, for old times' sake."

I really didn't care whose sake the dance was for. I took her in my paws and we became as one with each other and with the music.

All at once her eyes popped open, and she gasped, "Oh Hank, that is the most divine fiddle music I ever heard!"

"Is it now? How interesting, yes, but keep your eyes closed, my buttercup."

"Hank, what is the name of that song?"

The music stopped. "Uh, 'Just Friends,' " said the fox.

"Quiet, Frankie, I'll handle this. The tune is called 'Just Friends,' my darling, which doesn't really describe . . . ."

Her eyes popped open again. "Hank, I simply MUST find out where it's coming from!"

"Oh no, I don't think . . . ."

"WHO IS THAT FIDDLE PLAYER?"

"Oh, it's nobody you'd . . . ."

The music stopped and . . . I couldn't believe this part . . . that sneaking no-good egg-

stealing fox poked his smiling face around the trunk of the tree and he said . . . .

Here's what the sneaking, scheming, back-stabbing fox said. "Why, hello there, Miss Beulah! I was just a-sittin' here under this tree, a-playin' this old fiddle of mine, and I thought I heard the voice of an angel."

She gasped and held a paw to her heart. "Are YOU the fiddle player?"

"Uh, yes ma'am," he bowed to her, the wretch, "I have that little distinction. My name is Frankie the Fox, and I am at your service at any hour of the day or night."

I stepped in between them. "Excuse me, Beulah, if I might intrude here to make a . . . ."

She slipped past me. "Oh sir, your music is just divine!"

"Well, we thank you, ma'am. We try to do our best with the little gifts we have."

"Oh sir, you have a wonderful gift!"

Again, I tried to push between them. "Beulah, I think this would be a good time for me to point out . . . oof!" I never dreamed that sweet Beulah would stoop to throwing elbows, but she did.

"Ma'am," said the fox, "I'd be so proud if

you'd just touch my fiddle. I do believe it would make all my music, uh, that much sweeter."

"Why, I would just be . . . if you really thought . . . where should I touch it?"

The villain presented his fiddle. "Just place your fine, delicate, perfectly-made little paw right here."

She closed her eyes and placed her right paw on the fiddle. "Oh, this is so exciting! And Hank, it was all your idea."

"Well," I scowled at the fox, "up to a point it was. However . . . ."

She swooped over to me and gave me a peck on the cheek. "And there's your reward! Now, if you'll excuse me, I just must run and tell Plato! He'll be so excited!"

And with that, she went dashing off to find her stick-tailed friend who was off somewhere pointing tennis shoes.

"Beulah, wait! What about us? I still have important things to tell you. Beulah!"

She didn't hear me. I turned my attention to the fox and began considering three or four ways of . . . .

"Well, you sure fixed me up, Foxie."

"Son, that is one fine lady."

"Yes, I'm aware of that, and she's much too fine a lady to be drooling over a common hen house musician like you."

"She may be the best-looking collie gal I ever laid eyes on. You're a very, very lucky dog."

"I'm a lucky dog? She throws herself on you and your stupid fiddle, and then runs off to tell her bird dog boyfriend about it, *and I'M a lucky dog?* You've just ruined my life, is how lucky I am."

He gave me a puzzled look. "Son, you told me to play my fiddle, and I played my fiddle. You told me to charm that gal, and I charmed that gal."

"Yes, but I never told you to come out and take credit for it, just as though you'd actually done something. You idiot, she fell in love with your music, not me!"

He looked at his fiddle and shrugged. "You know, Hank, this fiddle music is kindly hard to predict. Sometimes it falls on deaf ears and sometimes it don't. A guy just has to try it out and see. If I was to try it again, I'd put a little less oomph on my bow."

"Well, you don't need to worry about that. There won't be another time. You're fired, you're through. You'll never work for me again, I'll see to that. Unless, of course, I want another broken heart, and in that case you'll be the first one on my list."

"Oh, uh shucks."

"So, thanks a lot, Frankie. In less than 12 hours' time, you've helped me lose my ranch, my job, my reputation, and now My One and Only True Love. If there's ever anything I can do for you, please don't hesitate to drop dead. And with that, I'll say goodbye. Forever."

"Oh?"

"Yes, and don't try to talk me out of it."

"Son, I wouldn't think of it."

"No, of course not, because you're such a selfish, heartless cad. You know very well that I have no place to go and that I'm a dog without a country, but do you care about that?"

"Well now, of course I care about that."

"No you don't. You're just saying that because you're a sneaking, scheming untrustworthy fox who can't be trusted. If you really cared, you'd . . . I don't know what you'd do, but you'd do something. But of course you won't because you don't care about anyone but yourself."

Frankie sighed and turned a pair of lazy eyes in my direction. "Son, would it help your disposition at all if we went to the hen house and got ourselves a nice big supper?"

I began pacing, as I often do when difficult decisions are pressing down upon me. I noticed that my stomach was growling.

"Frankie, we need to get one thing straight right here and now, and I mean bring it right out in the open."

"Uh huh."

"I'm no pushover."

"No, I figgered you weren't."

"For years they've tried to get me to sell out and compromise my principles, and every time the answer has been, 'No dice.' "

"I see."

"There are some things a dog just can't do without destroying his pride."

"Uh huh."

"So I'll accept your offer, but I'm doing it as a personal favor to you."

"Uh, thank you so much."

I dabbed at the moisture in the corners of my eyes. "Sometimes, Frankie, a guy just doesn't know how he can stand to live another day."

He patted me on the shoulder. "I know, son, but they tell me that the best cure for a broken heart is a dozen busted eggs."

"And you're suggesting that mere food could heal this terrible wound?"

"In a word, uh, yes."

My stomach growled again. "In that case, let's adjourn to the chicken house and let Miss Beulah feather her own nest."

And off we went to the chicken house, never suspecting that . . . well, you'll see.

CHAPTER
12

HEARTBROKEN AND SPRAYED, BUT A HERO TO THE END

On our way to the chicken house, we talked.

"Frankie, I was too good for her anyway."

"Um hmm."

"Any woman who'd chase after a bird dog is for the birds."

"I'm sure that's right."

"And, to be quite frank, Frankie, I don't even . . . ." Suddenly I fell to the ground with a terrible pain in my chest. "Holy smokes, I think my heart's cut half in two. I love her, Frankie, I can't get her off my mind, rush me to the chicken house!"

"Get up, son, I can't carry you."

121

I struggled to my feet. Holding a front paw over my heart, I limped onward, until at last we reached the chicken house. The sun had gone down. Darkness had fallen over the valley and, best of all, the chickens had gone to roost.

Frankie put his ear to the door and listened. When he straightened up, I saw that he was wearing that same old sly smile I had seen the night before.

"All's well. I'll go first and play. And then," he winked, "uh, let the feast begin."

"I'll be right behind you."

He cranked up his fiddle and slipped inside, and I followed a step or two behind. At that point, I began to notice that clouds had covered the full moon and that it was rather dark. Very dark. Pitch black.

In other words, this job would have to be done strictly on sound and feel. I could hear the hens' feet swishing across the floor as they got out of their nests and began to dance, and now and then a contented clucking sound came to my ears.

So far so good. I came to the first nest and gobbled two nice, fresh, juicy eggs. Already the pain in my heart had begun to slip away. Yes, this was an excellent cure.

I moved along and came to the next . . . this hen hadn't left her nest. Perhaps she was old, or Baptist and didn't believe in dancing. I would have to . . . .

Funny, I'd thought that all hens had feathers, not hair. I fumbled around in the darkness with my paws and . . . *this hen had hair.* That was a new one on . . . .

And a TAIL? A long tail with the hairs sticking straight out? Now, that beat it all. I had never heard of a chicken with hair and a tail.

And four legs? Hmmm. Very strange.

And, you know, the chicken house sure had a peculiar odor about it, almost like the smell of a . . . HUH?

WHOOOOOOSH! SPLAT! SSSSSSSSSS!

I stumbled through the darkness, gasping for breath and stepping on squawking hens. I tumbled out the door, and a moment later, Frankie tumbled out on top of me.

We both gagged and coughed and caught our respective breaths, but then we had to make fast tracks for the creek bottom, since the chickens were raising a terrible stink. So to speak. Noise, actually.

We ran for our lives and managed to reach the willows without being shot, collapsed on

124

the ground and panted for air. The air, by the way, smelled awful.

Frankie was the first to speak. "Son, I told you once before that you have a heavy touch with the chickens. What was it that went off in there?"

"Frankie, the best I can figger is that they've got egg-laying skunks on this ranch."

"Uh, no. The skunk might have been *stealin'* eggs, but he wasn't a-layin' eggs."

"Whatever. But I'm almost sure that there was a skunk in the nest."

"Yes, I think you could say that. And he did go off and you did take a direct hit."

"Yes, of course. It's all coming together now: the hair, the tail, the four feet, the strange odor, and then the whoosh sound. That *was* a skunk in there, Frankie, and I'll bet he was robbing eggs."

Frankie wrinkled up his nose and began backing away. "Son, this friendship has just been put to the test, and it has, uh, flunked. When you get to smellin' better, I hope you'll look me up. Nothing personal, but good night, goodbye, and good luck."

"Wait! Frankie? Why you, you . . . fair weather friend! You fickle fiddle-playing fox!

Go ahead and leave a friend just because he stinks, see if I care! I didn't like your smell either, so there!"

No answer. He was gone.

Sure was quiet out there. And kind of lonely. Very lonely. Holy smokes, I'd lost everything —my job, my girl, my friends, my gunny sack. I had no one to tell my troubles to, and nowhere to go.

I began walking up the creek, with my head and tail sunk so low that they almost met in the middle. I was hauling around all the cares of the world, fellers, and wondering if I could stand to drag myself through another night. But then . . . .

I heard a sound, a voice. I lifted my head and perked my ears, and noticed that I had been walking for an hour or more and had reached a point just down the creek from Slim's place.

I stopped and listened. There it was again. Yes, it was a voice, a faint voice, calling someone.

"Here boy! Come on home!"

Someone was out in the night, calling his dog. That only made me feel worse, knowing that there were people in the world who cared enough about their dogs to . . . .

There it was again, only this time . . .

"Hank, here boy! Here, Hank!"

Hank? Could there be TWO dogs named Hank on this creek? Surely . . . no! Someone was out in the night, calling for ME!

I went streaking towards the sound of the voice, and somehow the thought never occurred to me that the unknown party in the equation might be calling me for a date with THE FIRING SQUAD.

I'm a trusting soul, don't you know, and in the excitement of hearing my own name, I had forgotten that I had been seen the night before, running away from Sally May's chicken house with a two-faced, nest-robbing, fiddle-playing fox.

And so, like an innocent pup who has no knowledge of life's twisted path, I ran straight towards the two flashlight beams that probed the darkness along the creek.

And I was even foolish enough to bark and give them my exact position.

I heard the click-click of the pump shotgun, as one of the strangers threw a loaded shell into the chamber. Both flashlight beams swung around and punched me in the eyes. I came to a sudden stop.

It was at that moment that the awful truth hit me.

I had walked right into a trap, fellers. An ambush. A cruel conspiracy. They had me just where they wanted me, and it was all over but the shooting.

"Well," I said to myself, "Hold your head up, old son, and take it like a cowdog." I closed my eyes, held my head up, and waited for the ineffible . . . inedible . . . inevitable.

"Hey Loper, it's him! It's old Hank!"

"By gollies, it is! I thought he was a coyote at first."

Heavy footsteps came my way through the tall grass. I waited for the flash of light and the boom and the ineffible buckshot. But they didn't come.

Suddenly Slim and Loper were there in front of me, and . . . I cracked my eyes and saw smiles? I didn't want to be a sucker, but just in case those smiles were meant for me, I gave my tail a tentative wag.

"Hank, you old rascal, we've been looking all over this valley for you! Where have you been?"

I, uh, ran a paw across my mouth, just in case there might have been . . . just to spruce myself up for the, uh, company, because it's never a good idea to meet the public with a, uh, dirty face.

"We were scared that after you chased that fox off the ranch yesterday, he might have whupped up on you. Good dog, Hank, and welcome home!"

I could hardly believe my ears. This was too good to be true, and yet . . . .

Loper set his shotgun on the ground an crouched down. It appeared that he wanted to give me a hug, so I coiled my legs under me and flew into his awaiting arms. And also licked him on the face.

"Yeah, good dog, Hank. My wife is mighty proud of . . . shoo! My gosh, Hank, you smell worse than fifteen dead elephants! What in the world did you get into this time?"

He coughed and gagged and pushed me away.

Slim shifted his toothpick from one corner of his mouth to the other. "Smells a little like a skunk, don't it?"

"A *little?* Slim, this dog is a danger to the public health! Hank, you old fool, just once I wish you'd . . . oh, well, at least he's back home. Nothing ain't perfect, I guess."

"Not on this ranch, it ain't," said Slim.

Well, it turned out to be another triumphant homecoming for you-know-who, which was a bit more than I had dared to hope for. And here's how that happened.

Sure 'nuff, Loper had seen me and Frankie and Drover running away from the chicken house, and sure 'nuff, he had fired his shotgun in our direction.

But it had been our good fortune that Frankie the Fox had been *in the lead*, which meant that we dogs had appeared to be *chasing him off the ranch.*

Which hadn't been entirely an accident come to think of it. You see, I had suspected all along that . . . .

Well, shucks, look at the record. I had caught that sneaking, thieving Frankie the Fox in the act of robbing eggs and had run him off the ranch forever. I had gotten the hero's welcome I so richly deserved, and things had turned out right in the end.

And fellers, there's no better time to end a story than when things have turned out right, and there's no better place to end a story than at the end. And this is just about the end.

One last word and then I'll quit. You remember the parts of this story where I was supposedly robbing nests and eating raw eggs with that sneaking fox? Those passages were based on gossip and inconclusive reports.

In other words, I was misquoted. I would

appreciate it if you would go back through this book and scratch out those passages because, well, people might get the wrong idea.

Heads of Ranch Security do not, I repeat, DO NOT rob nests or eat raw eggs. Never. Ever.

Honest.

Cross my heart.

No kidding.

Thanks. See you around. And don't forget to cross out the naughty parts.

G.L. Holmes

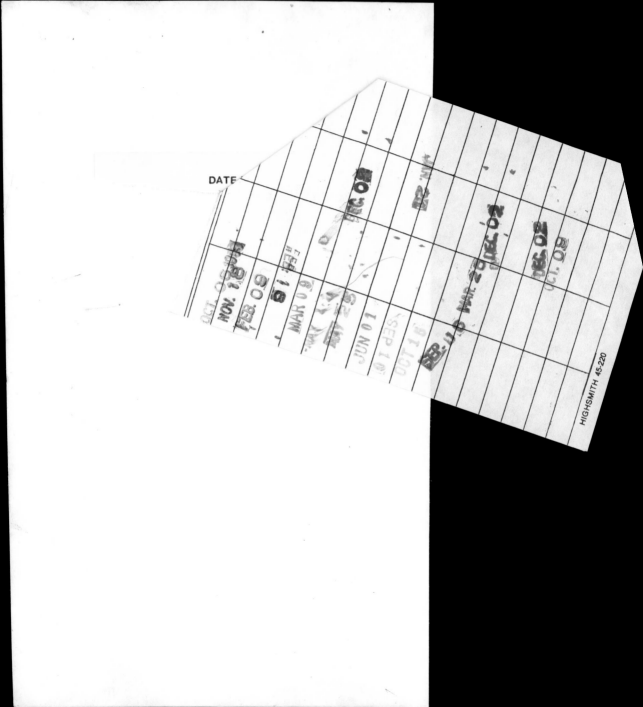

DATE

OCT. 06 2004
NOV. 18 09
FEB. 09
FEB. 16
MAR 09
MAY 14
MAY 29
JUN 01
SEP 16
SEP 10

DEC. 03

MAY 25

SEP. 11 9 MAR. 20 DEC. 02

DEC. 02

DEC. 02
OCT. 09

HIGHSMITH 45-220